"...and JUAN"

By
TERRY SHANNON

Illustrated by
CHARLES PAYZANT

ALBERT WHITMAN & COMPANY
CHICAGO   ILLINOIS

DEDICATION

With sincere appreciation this book is dedicated to
Senora Sara Estela Gutierrez because of her untiring
efforts to keep Mexican folk art alive and in its pure
form; to Senora Maria Elena Icaza Haase for the love
and help she has given many peasant children living on
the outskirts of Mexico City and for her kindness in
reading the manuscript; and to the potters of Mexico,
young and old, whose colorful work has brought pleasure to tourists from all over the world as well as to this
author and artist.

Terry Shannon and Charles Payzant
Hollywood, California

AUTHOR'S FOREWORD

This book was inspired by a gay striped flying horse of clay, made in the village of Metepec, Mexico. The horse is now a treasured part of the Shannon-Payzant folk art collection in their workshop and was used as a model for the pictures of Juan's horse.

Folk arts and crafts are being carried on in many villages throughout Mexico. A whole family may devote its time to turning out salable wares with even small children doing their bit to help.

Many families are noted for special wares of distinctive design and coloring. This may be true of an entire village.

In order to give variety to his illustrations, Mr. Payzant has used the shapes, designs and colors of the products of many artisans from many villages in addition to the very distinctive angels, animals, etc., created by the potters of Metepec.

Terry Shannon

"... and JUAN"

Golden heat spilled down from the sun onto the tiny Mexican village where Juan lived. All was quiet inside the adobe houses. All was quiet outside the adobe houses.

Everyone slept in the peaceful warmth of early afternoon, the time of the little sleep. Not a hen clucked. Not a rooster crowed. Even the goats and the burros dozed on the hillsides.

Sleeping in the patio just outside their house were Pedro, Pepito, Pancho, Pablo, and Juan.

When the sun moved along a little farther in the bright blue sky, their father stepped through the doorway of the house and called to them. "Come my sons, the time of sleeping is over. It is the time to work."

He stepped out into the patio. "Come Pedro,

Pepito, Pancho, Pablo . . . and Juan. Busy yourselves."

When Papa called his sons he always did it just that way, as though he suddenly remembered that Juan was part of the family.

Sometimes Juan wished Papa would forget altogether to say ". . . and Juan." If Papa said only "Pedro, Pepito, Pancho and Pablo," Juan could sleep a little longer or play a little longer.

Then there were other times when Juan wished very much that Papa wouldn't almost forget to add his name to the others as though it was hardly worth the effort.

But it was always the same, "Come my sons. Come Pedro, Pepito, Pancho, Pablo . . . and Juan."

Now at the sound of Papa's voice Pedro

pushed his big sombrero onto the back of his head from its resting place over his face. He blinked his eyes in the bright sunlight.

Pepito pushed back his sombrero and blinked.

Pancho pushed back his sombrero and blinked.

Pablo pushed back his sombrero and he too blinked his eyes.

And Juan gave a push to his sombrero, getting slowly to his feet with the others as he did so. A fringe of straight black hair showed beneath his big hat. White teeth gleamed from his brown face. He rubbed the sleep from big black eyes.

"Si, Papa," the five boys said. "Yes, Papa. We will busy ourselves."

Pedro, Pepito, Pancho and Pablo picked up

...'and Juan

7

the work they had put down earlier, the pots and jugs they were making.

And Juan went to a great mound of clay in the corner of the courtyard, to knead it with his bare feet.

Papa Sanchez was a potter. He made pots and jugs of clay. When he had the time he made gay animals and birds or beautiful angels or other figures of clay. Sometimes he made delicate and elaborate candle holders and incense burners for use on special days.

Pedro, Pepito, Pancho and Pablo, too, were potters. They made pots and jugs of clay. Once in a while when they had the time, they too made gay animals and other figures.

Papa had to sell many pots and jugs and animals and angels in the Market Place in the

8

City. He had to sell many things to supply his
family with their needs.

When business was good, Papa sometimes
had a few centavos or even a whole peso left
over to bury in the ground for safe keeping.

When business was bad, Juan and the others
contented themselves with smaller servings of
beans and fewer tortillas. They worked all the

harder in their little plot of ground to make the corn and beans and chili peppers grow.

Now Papa, Pedro, Pepito, Pancho and Pablo were busy with their pottery.

And Juan was busy preparing more clay for them, working out the loose gravel. Squishing the soft clay through his bare toes, Juan smiled. The tickle of the clay oozing about his ankles was like the soft wet licking of his puppy's tongue. It was fun to knead the clay, though it wasn't much fun when a pebble bruised his toe.

Then, kneading the clay this way and that, Juan's legs began to ache. His back and even his neck ached. Now it was not fun at all to knead the clay.

As he tramped out the pebbles, Juan longed

for the day he would spend more time working the clay with his hands than with his feet.

He would make gay animals and fat birds and beautiful angels and other figures. And when he had the time he might make a few pots and jugs.

Of course Juan was learning to become a potter, trying to shape and mold the clay as

Papa did. Already he had made some little animals. He had made some tiny pots and jugs.

These Papa had allowed him to paint with gay colors just as Papa himself and the other boys painted their handiwork.

Papa, however, had not taken any of Juan's pottery to the Market Place to sell to the touristas and people from other villages. Maria, Juan's sister, used them for toys.

Somehow, none of the things Juan had made were very good. Pedro, Pepito, Pancho and Pablo sometimes laughed at him and his efforts. "What a funny pig," they would say. Or, "Your rabbit looks like a burrito."

And, too, they often said, "Why do you not forget about the animals and birds? Make only the pots and jugs. They are easier."

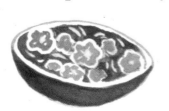

12

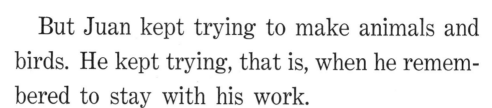

But Juan kept trying to make animals and birds. He kept trying, that is, when he remembered to stay with his work.

Seldom could he sit still long enough to finish anything. He would no sooner start to shape an animal than the bleating of Rosita, the goat, would fill his ears. Before he knew it, he was running off to play with her.

Or he would go chasing after butterflies or birds or run off to play with El Burrito, the baby burro. When he came back to his work the clay was too dry and he would have to start over. And quite often he had trouble making the clay into the shape he wanted.

"When will I be able to make things that you will sell in the Market Place, Papa?" Juan sometimes asked.

14

"In the little now," Papa would answer, meaning after a while. Or "Manana," which meant some future day. Sometimes Papa would say, "When the moon is right the clay will work itself in your hands."

But mostly Papa said, "When you busy yourself with the clay instead of running off to play with Rosita or over the hills after butterflies or birds or burros. You spend more of your time playing with the live animals than you do trying to make ones of clay."

On one day each week Papa, Mama, Maria, Pedro, Pepito, Pancho, Pablo and Juan went to the great city to sell the Sanchez pottery.

"Si," Papa would say to people who asked, "Yes, the pots and jugs, the animals and other figures are all made by us. They are made by

15

me and my sons, Pedro, Pepito, Pancho and Pablo."

This was the *one* time Papa didn't add Juan's name, after a pause, to the rest. And this was the *one* time Juan especially wanted to hear it. He wanted to hear Papa say, "Yes, we are the potters. Me and my sons Pedro, Pepito, Pancho, Pablo . . . and Juan."

Until that would happen Juan felt somehow he wasn't quite as important a part of the family as were Pedro, Pepito, Pancho and Pablo.

Early one morning, as he often did, Juan went with Mama and Maria to the river.

Here, with the other women and children, they bathed. Then while Mama and Maria beat and slapped and scrubbed the dirty clothes against flat stones until they were clean and white, Juan dug some clay from the river bank.

The clay was fine and free of grit. How good it felt in his hands. He rolled it into a round ball.

"The very thing," Juan said to himself, his eyes lighting on a turtle sunning itself. "I will make a turtle."

Slapping and working carefully Juan made a hollowed out place in the lump of clay, humping it up to look like the turtle's shell.

Butterflies flew past but Juan paid no attention.

Molding and shaping the clay, Juan felt as though it were coming to life in his hands. Birds twittered and sang, circling about him, but he paid no attention.

After a great deal of reshaping, he had the body so that it suited him. Patting and pushing and pulling, he gave his turtle four legs.

Goats bleated on the little hills and burros wandered nearby, but Juan paid no attention.

Rolling some clay into a short rope he divided it in two. From one piece he made a tail. From the other he made a head. He attached them

to the body he had shaped. His fingers felt at
home with the clay as he gave a final pat to
his work.

Not once had he run off. Not once had he
put his turtle down until it was finished.

He put it to dry in the shade until he left
the river with Mama and Maria. When he got
home he put it on the roof of the house. How

fine it looked drying there beside the pots and jugs and animals his brothers and Papa had made.

All the next day, the sun beat down upon Juan's turtle. The day after that, too, the sun drew out the moisture from it. On the third day, it was dry enough to paint.

Papa, Pedro, Pepito, Pancho and Pablo each took something from the rooftop to paint. And Juan took down his turtle.

With bold strokes of the brush Juan painted it, giving it a brilliant coat of many colors. His turtle was a thing of wondrous splendor.

Papa and the others put their pots and jugs into a little brick oven to bake. And Juan put his turtle into the little oven to bake.

When it had been fired long enough and the

20

bricks were cool, Juan proudly took his turtle from the oven.

Pedro, Pepito, Pancho and Pablo did not laugh at Juan's work this time. "It is a fine turtle!" they said.

And Papa said, "Si. Yes, it is a fine turtle. A very gay animal. Tomorrow is market day and we will take it with us to sell!"

Juan beamed, pleasure glowing in his black eyes at this praise not only from Papa but from his brothers. At last he had made something Papa thought good enough to sell in the Market Place. He was a potter with the others, Juan thought happily.

With joy in his heart he ran to put his bright turtle with the other things Papa had ready for the City.

As he ran, the turtle slipped from his hands. It went smashing to the ground where it broke in tiny pieces. Gazing in anguish at the broken bits of his precious turtle, two fat tears spilled from Juan's eyes and rolled down his cheeks.

"A potter handles his wares with great care," Papa said, shaking his head sadly. "It takes much patience to be a potter for our wares break easily."

The others chatted gaily over their supper, planning for the journey to the City. Juan ate his beans in silence. As silently, he went to sleep on his straw mat.

The shivery excitement of early dawn on market day was dimmed for Juan when he remembered his broken turtle. Soon, however, something so momentous happened that he forgot even this great sadness.

"Come," Papa said when Pedro, Pepito, Pancho, Pablo and Juan went out to ready the burro for the trip to the City. "Today we ride the bus!"

Shaking with excitement himself, Papa smiled broadly at the effect this announcement had on his family. Never had they had such an adventure. And the centavos it would cost for

all of them to ride! Juan was stunned at the very thought.

The blue and white bus chugged along over the hills to and from the great city on certain days of the week. It passed Juan's village as it went.

Juan could not read the name its proud owner had painted on it. But many times he had seen the letters on the bus as it went puffing and snorting on its way. "Mi amor eres tu," the letters spelled.

"You are my love," the words meant. Juan had heard the driver tell Papa so, one day, . when he had stopped to ask Papa for a jug of water. Juan had even reached out and touched this great machine.

They were all ready and waiting when the bus came by on this very special occasion. Papa flagged it down. A little fear came welling up in Juan's mind as they climbed on and Papa counted out the centavos into the driver's hand. It was one thing to see the bus lurching on its way down the road but it was another to get on it and ride.

Two by two they sat down. Mama sat with Papa, holding Maria on her lap. Next came Pepito beside Pedro, Pablo beside Pancho . . . and Juan in the seat behind.

Juan shut his eyes tight and hung on as the bus leapt forward. He opened them slowly, looking out the window with new found courage. He was perfectly safe and sound. His fear soon gave way to an ever increasing thrill of delight.

Now and then they stopped along the way for other villagers who came crowding into the bus with their wares for market. They passed many people walking the long way or riding on burros, just as Juan and his family usually did.

Once they stopped while the driver fed and

watered the bus from two large cans. "The bus is like the animal," Juan said to himself. "It must be fed and watered. It must eat and drink."

It seemed to Juan that the bus fairly flew over the road. It went much faster than the burros. "It's like a horse," he thought. "It flies so fast over the countryside. The bus is like a flying horse."

Suddenly Juan had a wonderful idea. He would make a flying horse, a gay striped clay horse with wings.

He would make it in time to be blessed when it was the day of the Blessing of the Animals. Then, surely, it would not get broken. Surely, it would sell in the Market Place.

Usually it took them a long, long time to get to market. In the bus it seemed that they had no sooner started than they were there.

"It is a thing of wonder," Papa said as they got out of the bus. "But it is too fast. Better

I like to take the longer time, to visit on the way with other villagers."

Juan thought it a most magical journey, quite the most wonderful of any he had taken with Papa to the City.

Papa, Pedro, Pepito, Pancho and Pablo arranged their pottery on straw mats under a canopy in the open air. Mama visited with other women while Maria played nearby.

And Juan was free to wander about the crowded plaza. Shyly he threaded his way between the stalls looking at the sombreros, the baskets, the serapes and rebozos and all the other things people had brought from distant villages.

There were tempting fruits and vegetables of many kinds and many colors. His mouth watered at sight of some plump ripe reddish-golden bananas.

There was so much to see, so much to do. Following the bird man with his tall stack of cages, Juan's eyes caught sight of a toy man. He turned in delight to follow him. Laughing at tiny dolls dangling from a stick Juan jumped up and down, pretending that he too was dangling on a string from a stick.

It was a long day, a day packed with strange fun and laughter. On the way home Juan fell asleep, his head filled with jumbled dreams of birds and toys, fruits and sweets.

The next day Juan remembered the wonderful idea he'd had on the bus, to make a flying horse. He took a lump of moist clay in his hands. Just as he had done with his turtle he slapped and worked it carefully.

34

Again molding and shaping the clay, he felt
as though it were coming to life in his hands.
Butterflies flew past but Juan didn't look up.
Goats bleated from the little hills but Juan
scarcely heard them.

Birds sang in the trees. Hens clucked. The
rooster crowed. The dog ran past chasing the
burro. Still Juan worked on.

When his horse had a body and four legs, a head and a great wide mane, Juan rested a moment. "Now I must give my horse wings so that it can fly," he said.

With fingers now tired and aching he made wings and attached them firmly to the body of his horse.

There, it was finished!

"It is good," Papa said. "You have finished making your horse even though the butterflies flew past and the goats bleated and the burros called."

Papa looked more closely at Juan's horse. "It is a fine animal," he said. "The moon was right and the clay worked itself for you."

Pedro, Pepito, Pancho and Pablo looked at Juan's horse and said, "It is a good one. It looks like a horse." And they did not laugh, they only smiled friendly smiles at Juan.

Proudly Juan put his treasure on the rooftop. After a few days when the warm sun had dried it enough, he took his horse down and painted it.

He painted its head red and its mane yellow. He gave it a purple tail and green legs. On its

body he daubed green, yellow and red paint. He striped its wings with purple, green, red and yellow.

When Juan finished, he had a very gay flying horse. He looked at it in delight for a moment before gently placing it in the little brick oven to bake.

Before the sun had hidden its face for the night, the firing was through, the bricks cooling.

"It is a most wonderful flying horse," Papa said as Juan, holding his breath in anticipation, took it from the oven. "We will take it to market to sell next market day." Juan's heart thumped with joy at Papa's words.

Pedro, Pepito, Pancho and Pablo crowded around in admiration. "It is a very gay animal," they all agreed. "A beautiful flying horse."

"It can fly faster than the bus," Juan said shyly, unused to such praise.

But Juan himself did not fly as he went to put his horse down. He walked carefully, holding it with his two hands. He gazed at it lovingly, pride shining from his eyes. Secretly he liked it better than any of the animals his brothers or Papa had made.

Early in the morning of the day of the Bless-

ing of the Animals everyone was even busier than usual. "Come, my sons," Papa said. "We must make beautiful our real live animals."

Painting some with bright paint, they adorned others with garlands of flowers.

"Stand still, my little burrito," Juan said to a tiny burro as he put a wreath of flowers around its neck. "You must be beautiful to receive the blessing."

Mama and Maria, Papa, Pedro, Pepito, Pancho and Pablo led the gayly decorated animals through the village to the churchyard.

And Juan followed, clutching his gay flying horse tightly in his hands.

On the way they were joined by other villagers with their pet birds, their chickens and turkeys and dogs and goats and pigs and burros until there was a great parade.

Juan carried his horse so carefully that not once did it slip from his hands. The priest smiled gently at the solemn-faced small boy standing before him as Juan held up his gay horse to be blessed.

"But Juan," the priest said, "the Blessing of the Animals is for live animals. You have a little horse of clay."

"Oh, please, Padre," Juan begged, desire making him bold. "Please allow my little flying horse to be blessed with the others. Then I am sure he will be sold in the Market Place. He is my first to go to market!"

The priest smiled. "Well, I suppose there is no harm in it," he said. He went on with the ceremony, blessing Juan's clay horse as well as the live animals.

The next day in the City, Juan helped Papa and the others set out their wares on the mats. His flying horse had not got broken on the way. With a pleased smile, Juan put it a little to one side of the pots and jugs and animals and angels his brothers and Papa had made.

People came and went, looking, shopping, bargaining.

Some touristas came. They bought pots and jugs made by Pedro, Pepito, Pancho and Pablo. They bought pots and jugs made by Papa.

But it seemed that no one wanted Juan's flying horse. Or perhaps they did not see it. That must be it, Juan thought. He moved it forward a little on the mat. Maybe now it could be seen better by the shoppers.

Other touristas came and bought some of Papa's animals and birds and some of Papa's angels.

Juan watched hopefully, then forlornly, as they made their purchases and went away without choosing his horse.

The day wore on but still no one bought the gay little horse Juan had made. Juan stayed close by Papa's side. Today the bird man, the toy man and all the other exciting things in the Market Place held no attraction for him. He wanted only the excitement of seeing his clay horse sold.

All day, strange villagers and touristas stopped at Papa's stall. Some bought things, others only looked and visited. But no one bought Juan's horse of clay.

"Come my sons, the day is over," Papa said

when the sun had crossed the sky. "We must pack up for our journey home."

Juan was filled with bitter disappointment as Papa began packing the things that had not been sold. Why had no one bought his wonderful flying horse?

"Oh please wait!" a tourista said, rushing up to Papa's stall. "I would like to buy something."

Juan's hopes rose again as Papa unpacked the things and placed them on the mat.

The tourista bought an elegant candle holder and an incense bowl ringed round with angels. A lump came up in Juan's throat as the woman turned as though to leave.

Eyes filling with tears, Juan turned his head so the others would not see. Then he held his breath as the woman caught sight of his little horse.

"Oh! That gay little horse with wings!" she exclaimed. "How charming! I must have that!"

Juan's heart nearly stopped beating with relief. He brushed the tears from his eyes the better to watch the woman count the centavos into Papa's hand. At last someone wanted the splendid horse he had made. His beautiful gay flying horse was sold!

"Do you make all these things yourself?" the tourista asked Papa.

"Si," Papa said. "Yes." Now Juan's heart pounded in his ears until he could scarcely hear. Straining, he listened to Papa's voice. "Yes, we are the potters," Papa said. "Me and my sons, Pedro, Pepito, Pancho, Pablo and Juan."

Papa hadn't even paused the way he always did when he said ". . . and Juan." He linked Juan right with the others. Papa put his hand on Juan's shoulder and smiled at him. Juan smiled back.

The familiar words took on new meaning for Juan. He felt as though he *really belonged*. He was now a potter with Papa and his brothers. Papa had said so.

White teeth gleamed from Juan's brown face as his happy smile grew even broader. And Juan's big black eyes sparkled as Papa's words still rang in his ears, "Yes, we are the potters. Me and my sons Pedro, Pepito, Pancho, Pablo and Juan."

Pedro
Pepito
and Juan
Pablo
Pancho